Stuck in the Mud: Search and Rescue

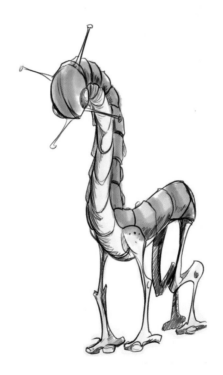

by Jason M. Burns

illustrated by Dustin Evans

 TORCH GRAPHIC PRESS

Published in the United States of America by Cherry Lake Publishing Group
Ann Arbor, Michigan
www.cherrylakepublishing.com

Reading Adviser: Beth Walker Gambro, MS, Ed., Reading Consultant, Yorkville, IL

Book Designer: Book Buddy Media

Torch Graphic Press is an imprint of Cherry Lake Publishing Group.

Library of Congress Cataloging-in-Publication Data has been filed and is available at catalog.loc.gov

Cherry Lake Publishing Group would like to acknowledge the work of the Partnership for 21st Century
Learning, a Network of Battelle for Kids. Please visit http://www.battelleforkids.org/networks/p21 for
more information.

Printed in the United States of America
Corporate Graphics

TABLE OF CONTENTS

Mission log: August 03, 2055.

Today we are headed north to visit what Dad calls a "special" kind of volcano. As someone who finds all volcanoes special, I can't wait to check them out. I wonder what kinds of Martians would live nearby? My friend, Daniela, is excited to analyze the soil in this part of the planet as well. We are eager to pack up our gear and get this latest adventure started.

—Malcolm Thomas

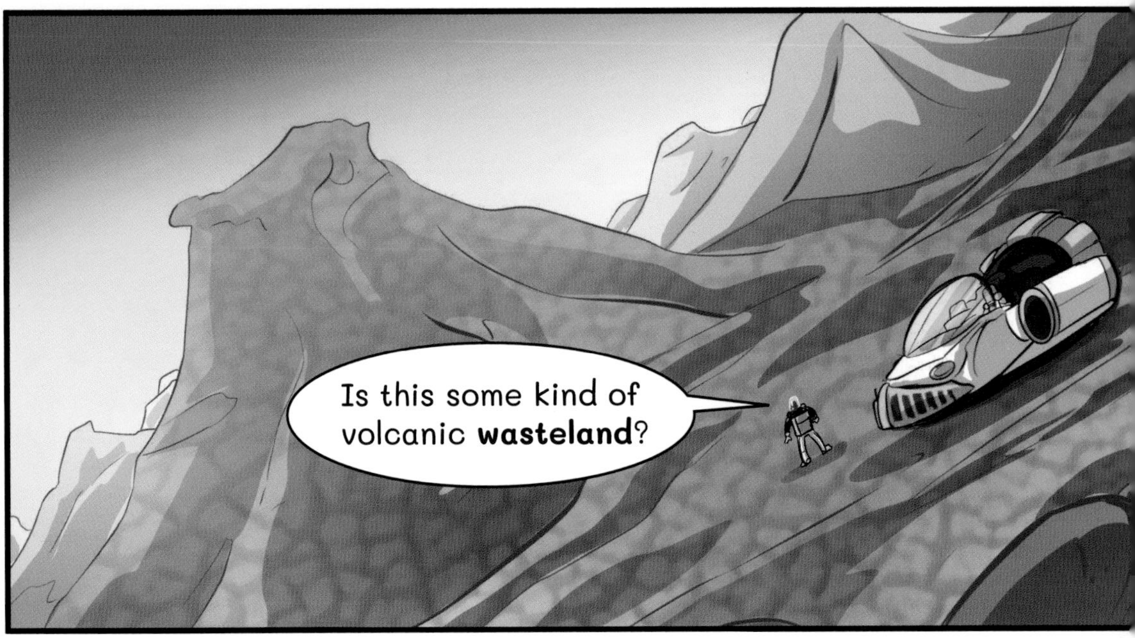
Is this some kind of volcanic **wasteland**?

MARS FACT

The biggest volcano in our solar system is Olympus Mons. It is located on Mars. It is about the size of the state of Arizona.

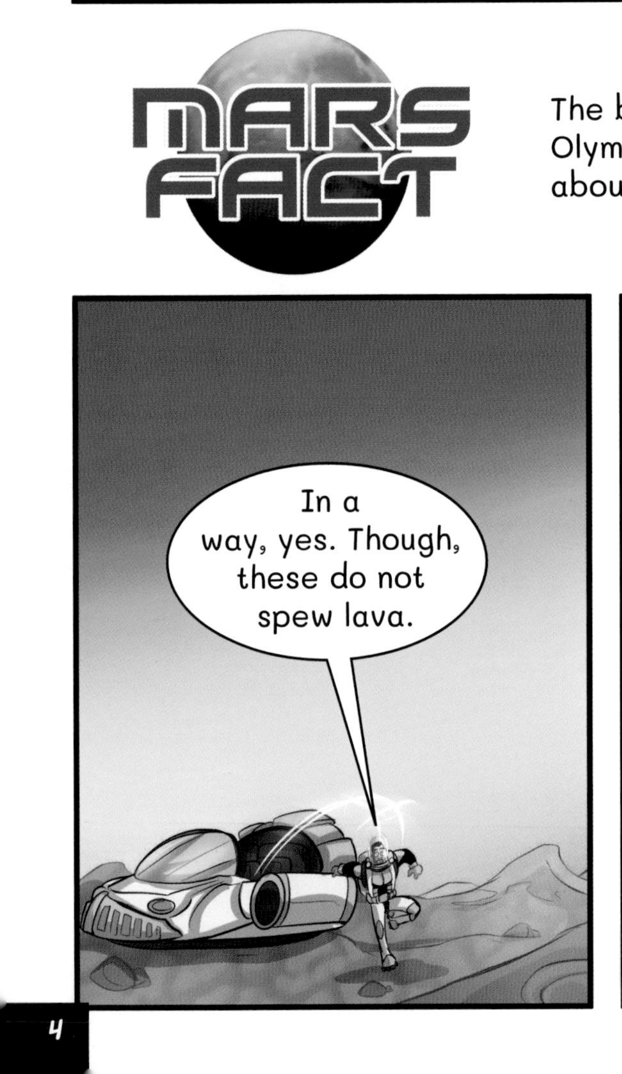
In a way, yes. Though, these do not spew lava.

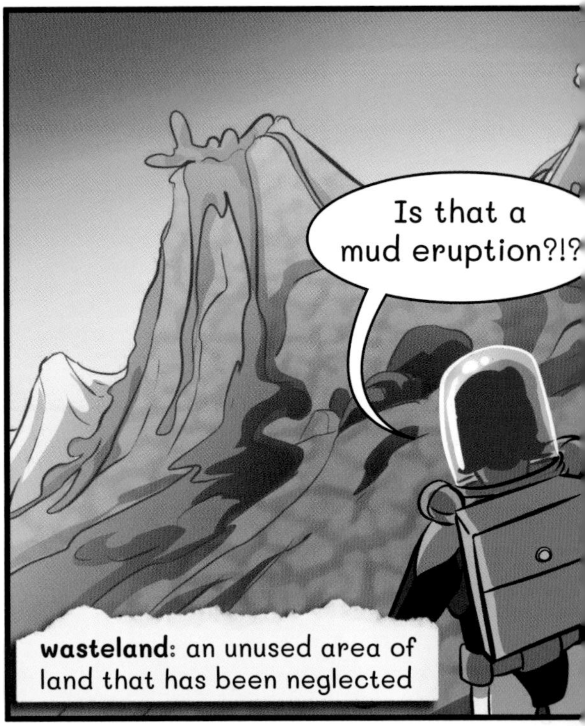
Is that a mud eruption?!?
wasteland: an unused area of land that has been neglected

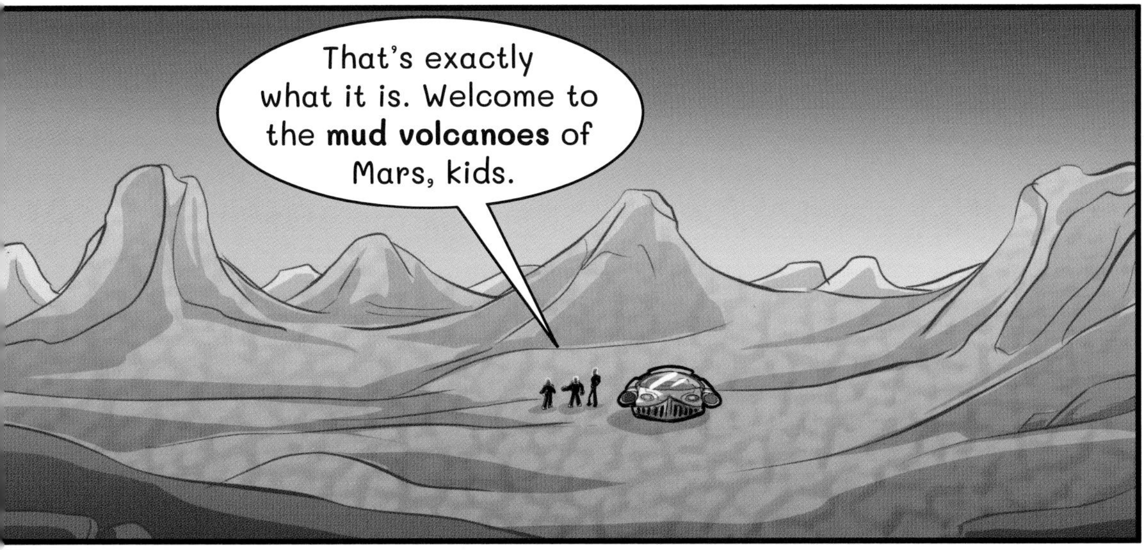
That's exactly what it is. Welcome to the **mud volcanoes** of Mars, kids.

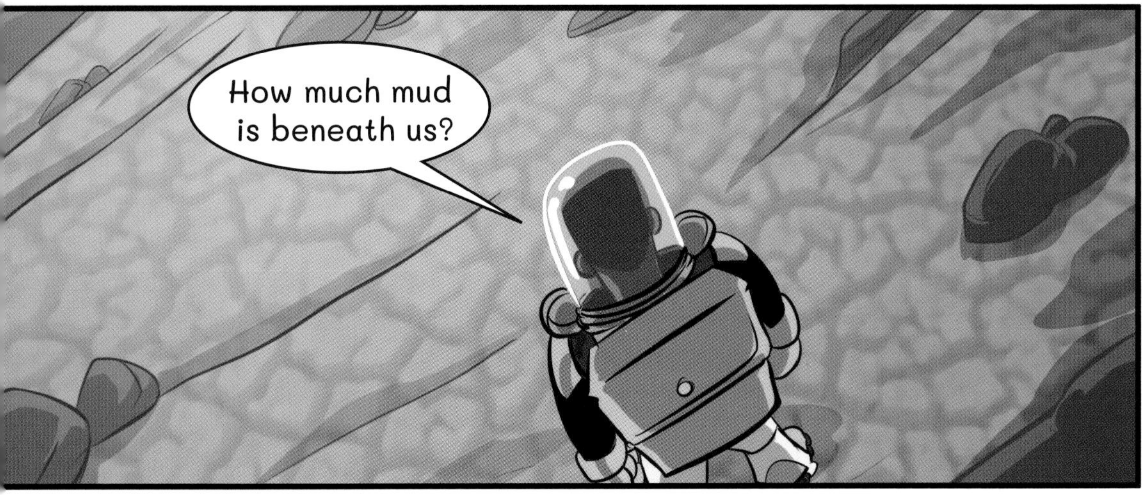
How much mud is beneath us?

MARS FACT

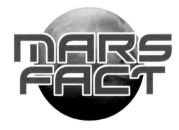

rover *Curiosity* discovered
the soil on Mars has 2 percent
er by weight. That means that,
day, astronauts could extract
er from the land.

mud volcanoes: vents in the ground that erupts hot mud

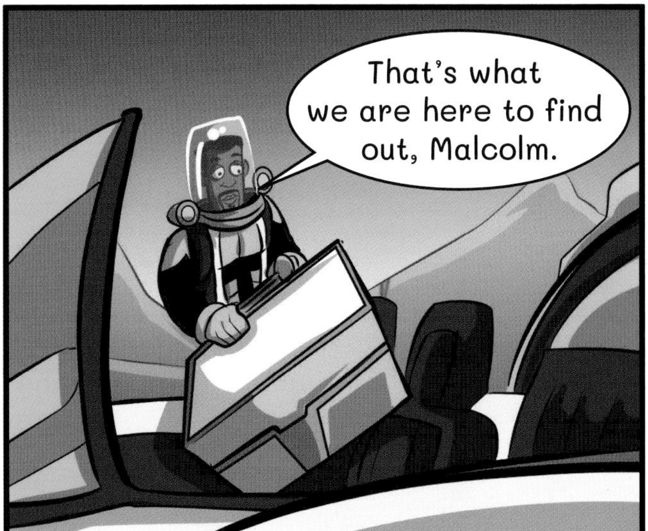
That's what we are here to find out, Malcolm.

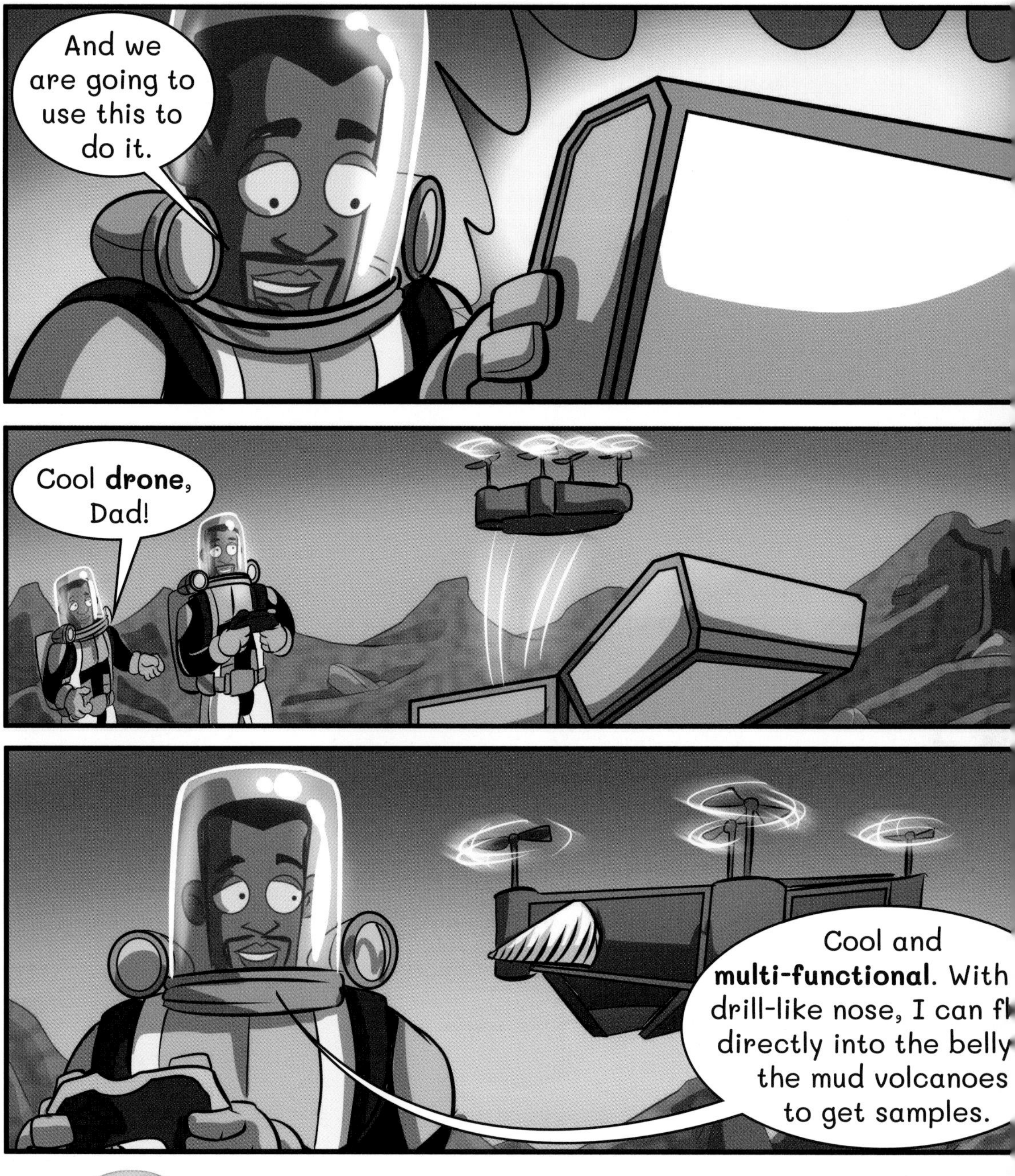
And we are going to use this to do it.
Cool **drone**, Dad!
Cool and **multi-functional**. With drill-like nose, I can fl directly into the belly the mud volcanoes to get samples.

MARS FACT

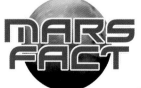

A regular drone could not fly on Mars. This is becaus of the planet's unique atmosphere. Mars has a much thinner atmosphere than Earth. Special **modificatio** are made to drones that make flight on Mars possib

drone: a small flying vehicle that is controlled from the ground

multi-functional: capable of performing various tasks

modifications: changes to something

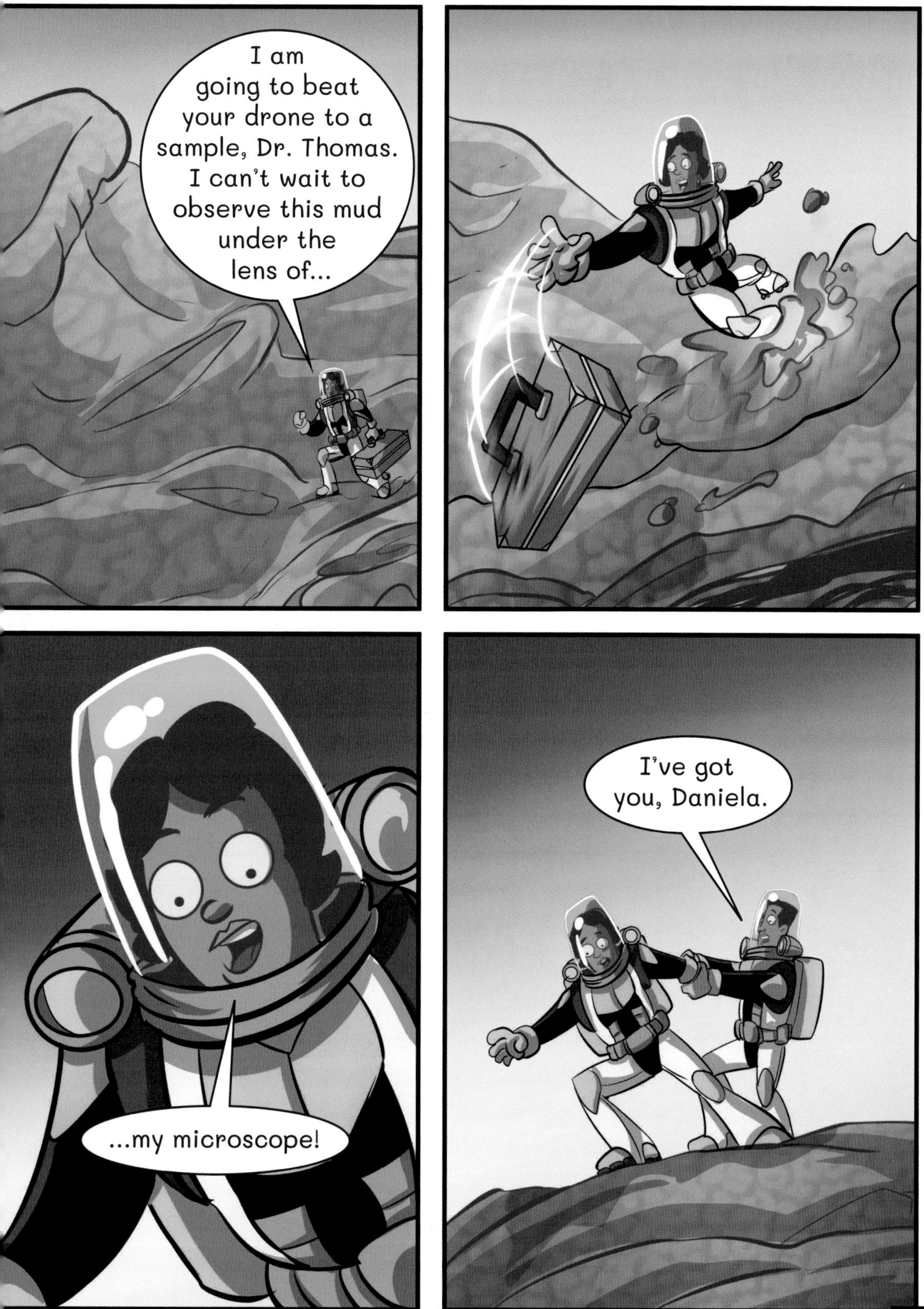
I am going to beat your drone to a sample, Dr. Thomas. I can't wait to observe this mud under the lens of...
...my microscope!
I've got you, Daniela.

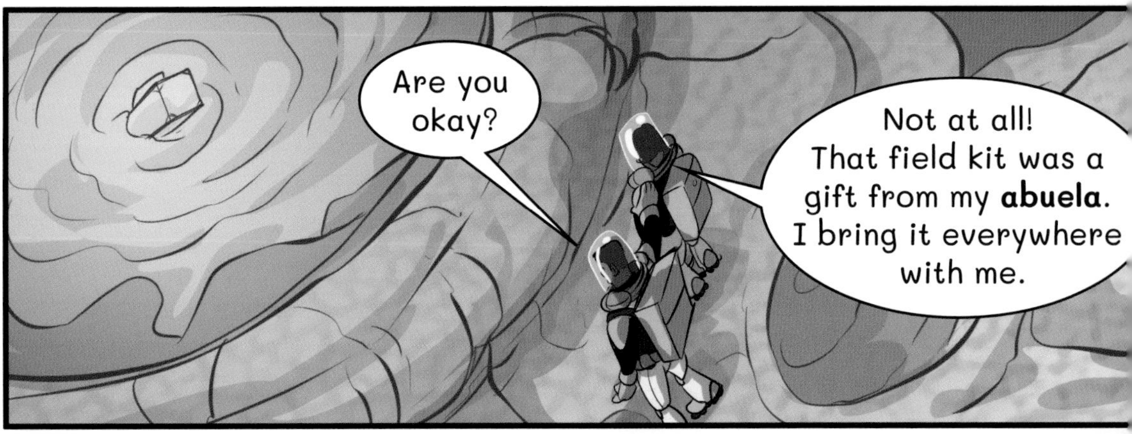
Are you okay?
Not at all! That field kit was a gift from my **abuela**. I bring it everywhere with me.

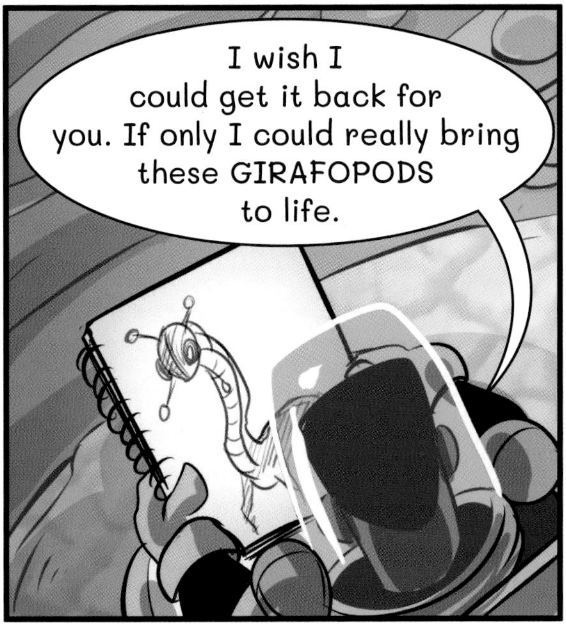
I wish I could get it back for you. If only I could really bring these GIRAFOPODS to life.

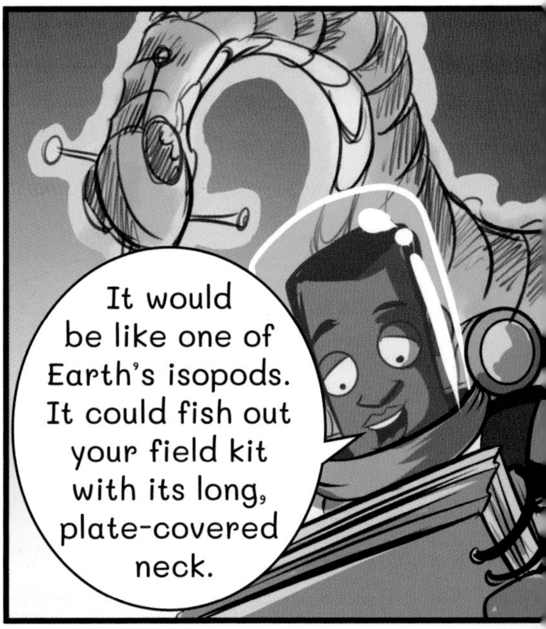
It would be like one of Earth's isopods. It could fish out your field kit with its long, plate-covered neck.

SCIENCE FACT

Isopods are creatures related to crustaceans, such as shrimp and crabs. They live in water and on land. There are 10,000 different species of isopods on Earth. The largest is the Bathynomus giganteus. It can grow up to 16 inches (0.4 meters) in length.

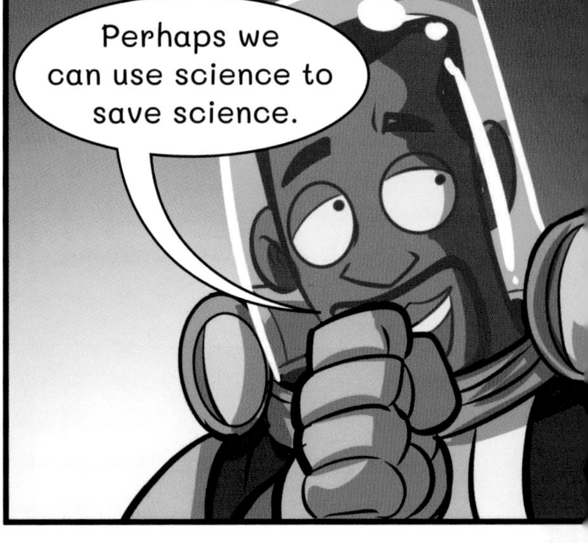
Perhaps we can use science to save science.

abuela: grandma in Spanish

THE CASE FOR SPACE

Theories about mud volcanoes on Mars are relatively new. Scientists used to think that the volcanoes erupted with lava. Now, though, they think that some of the "lava" was actually mud.

•Scientists believe that many volcanoes located in the planet's northern **hemisphere** are mud volcanoes.

•There are many mud volcanoes on Earth. One is at Yellowstone National Park.

•Mars is extremely cold. Mud does not move the same way there as it does on Earth.

•Scientists have **mimicked** the conditions found on Mars in a laboratory. To their surprise, mud on Mars is similar to lava from volcanoes on Earth.

•Researchers believe that mud would freeze very quickly on Mars. This is due to the low **atmospheric pressure**. But the low pressure wouldn't stop it from flowing.

•The mud would freeze from the outside in. This would allow the warm interior to break through the newly-formed crust. Then it would keep flowing down the slope of the volcano.

theories: ideas used to explain something

hemisphere: the top or bottom half of a planet

mimicked: imitated

atmospheric pressure: pressure created by the weight of the planet's atmosphere; on Earth, the higher you travel in the sky, the lower the pressure

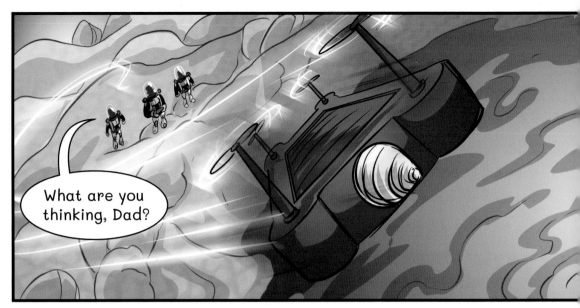

What are you thinking, Dad?

Well, if I can fly the drone into the mud and beneath the field kit...

...in theory, I should be able to fly it out on the drone's back.

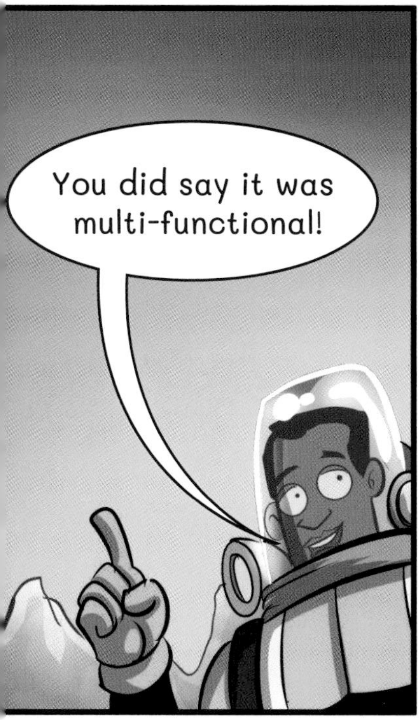
You did say it was multi-functional!

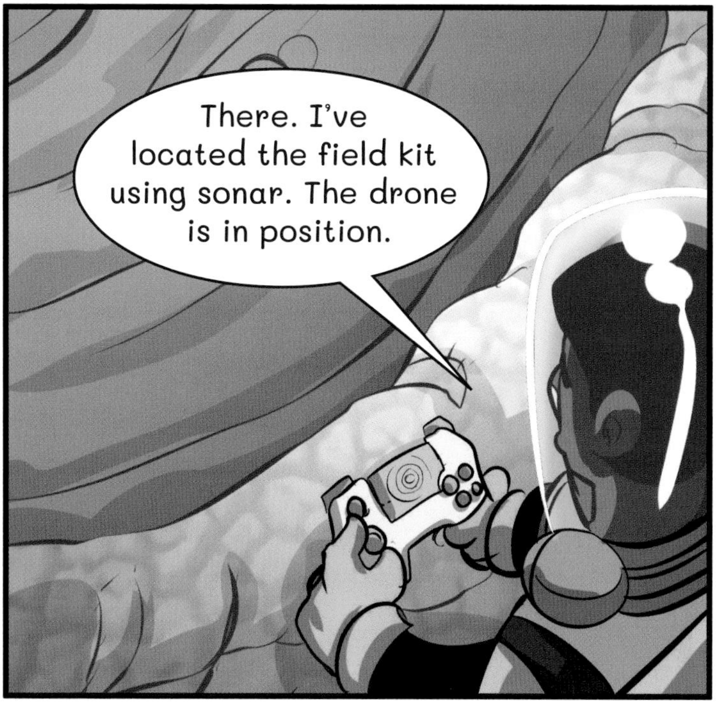
There. I've located the field kit using sonar. The drone is in position.

SCIENCE FACT

Sonar stands for Sound Navigation and Ranging. It works by sending out sound pulses which can identify the size and distance of objects. On Earth, dolphins use sonar to identify objects hundreds of yards away.

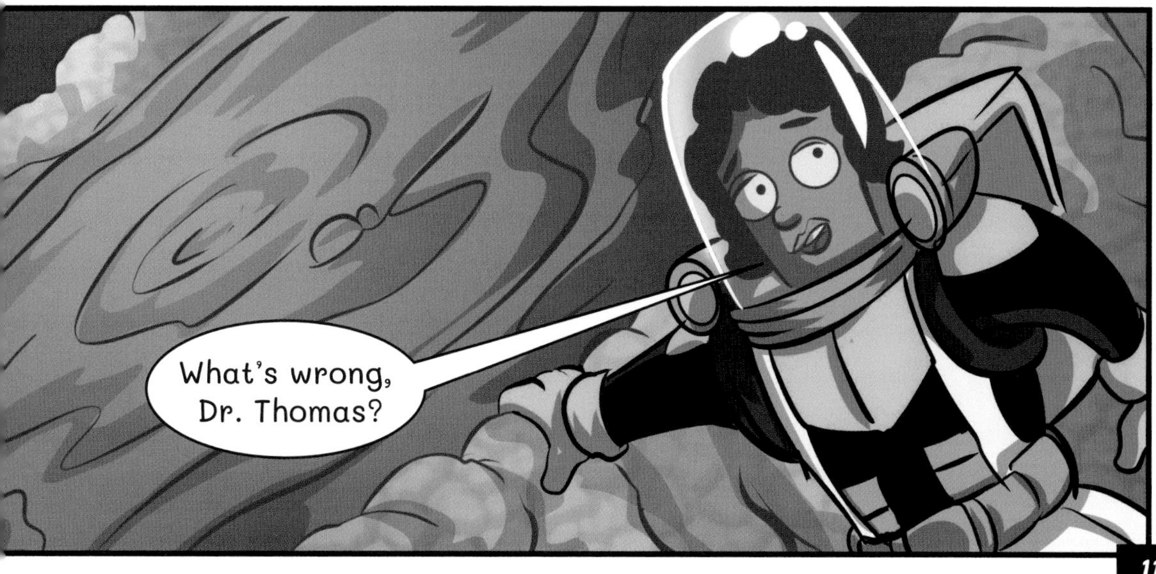
What's wrong, Dr. Thomas?

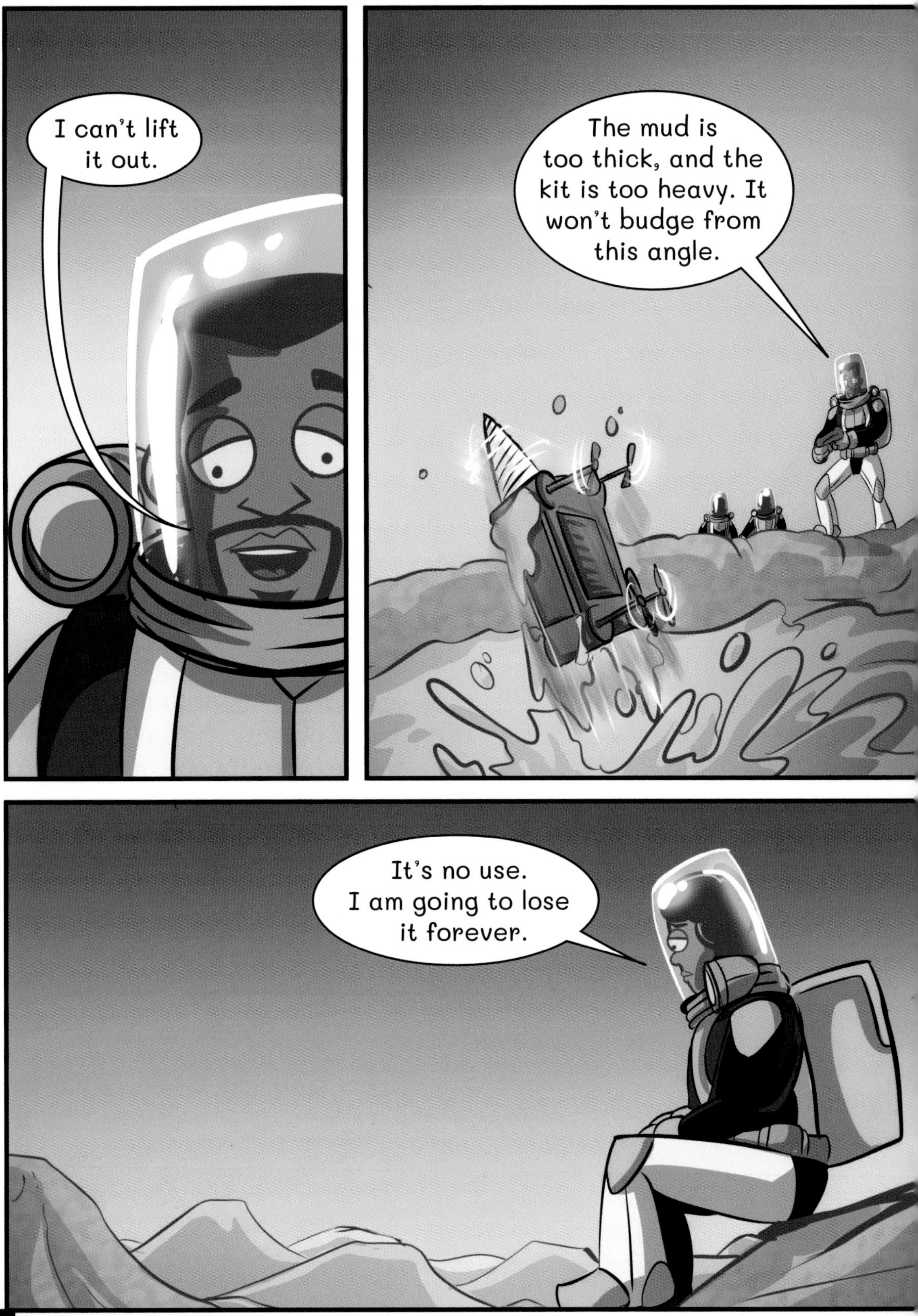
I can't lift it out.
The mud is too thick, and the kit is too heavy. It won't budge from this angle.
It's no use. I am going to lose it forever.

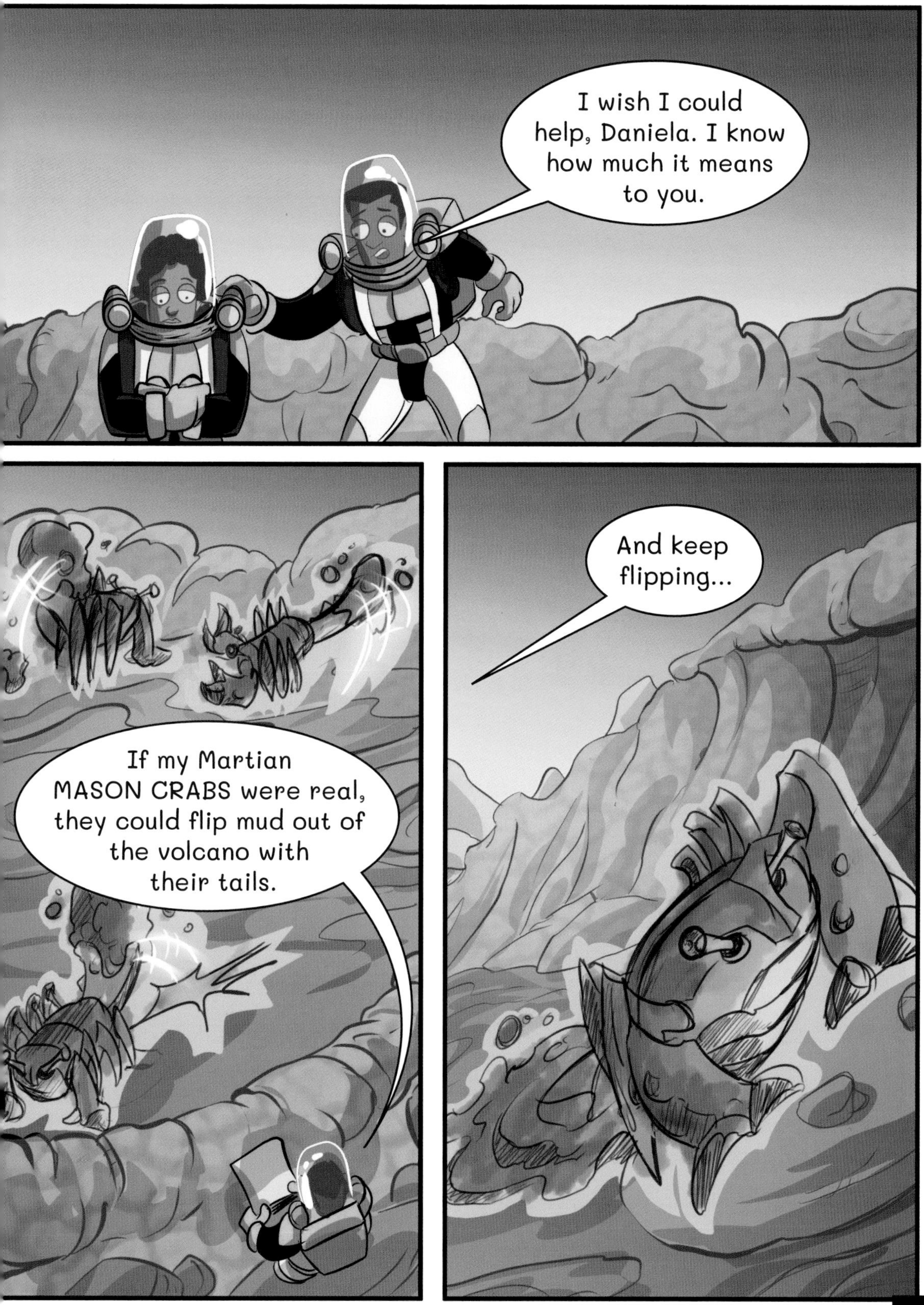

I wish I could help, Daniela. I know how much it means to you.
If my Martian MASON CRABS were real, they could flip mud out of the volcano with their tails.
And keep flipping...

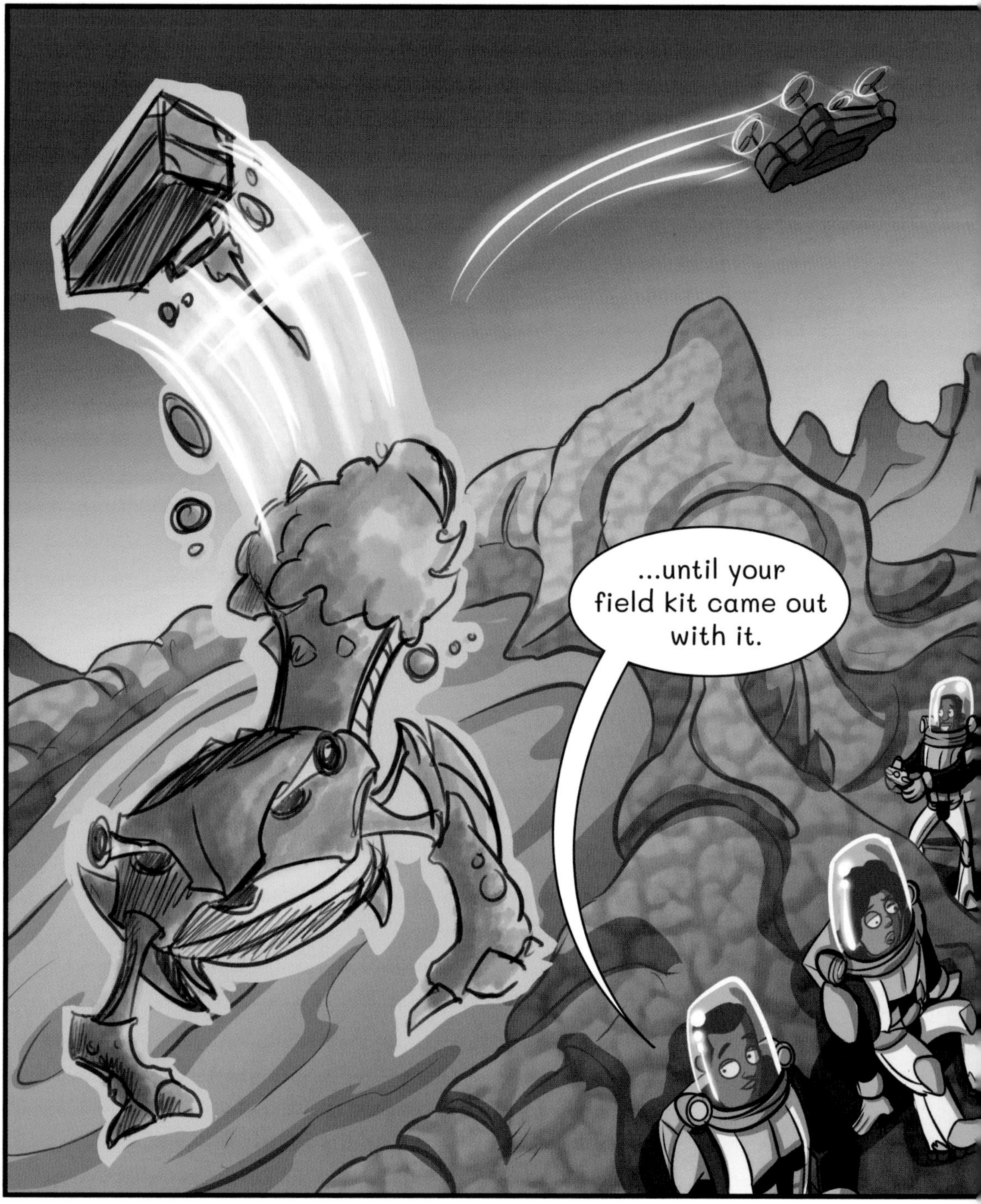
...until your field kit came out with it.

SCIENCE FACT

Beavers slap their flat tails against th
surface of the water. This warns othe
beavers of approaching predators.

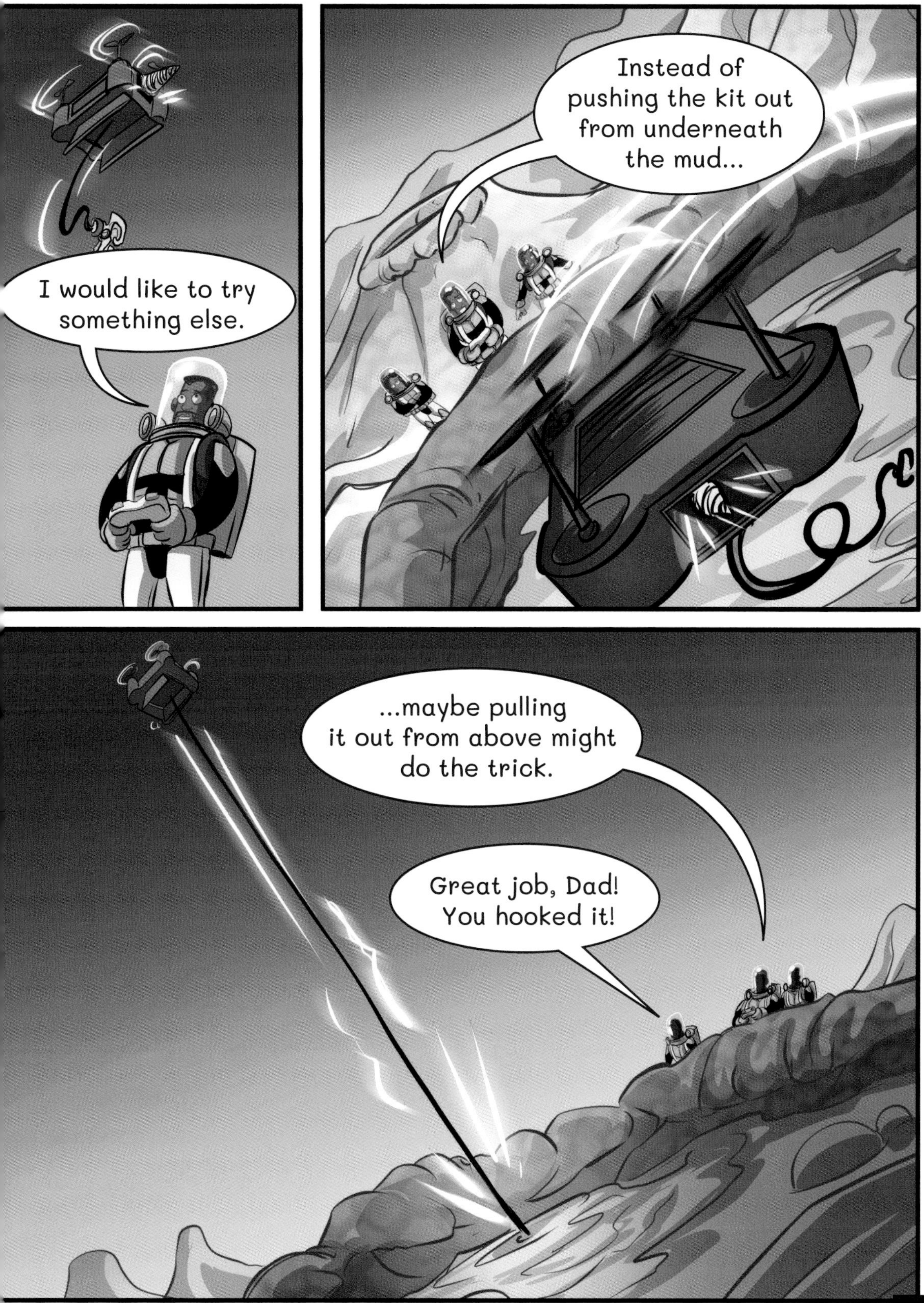
I would like to try something else.
Instead of pushing the kit out from underneath the mud...
...maybe pulling it out from above might do the trick.
Great job, Dad! You hooked it!

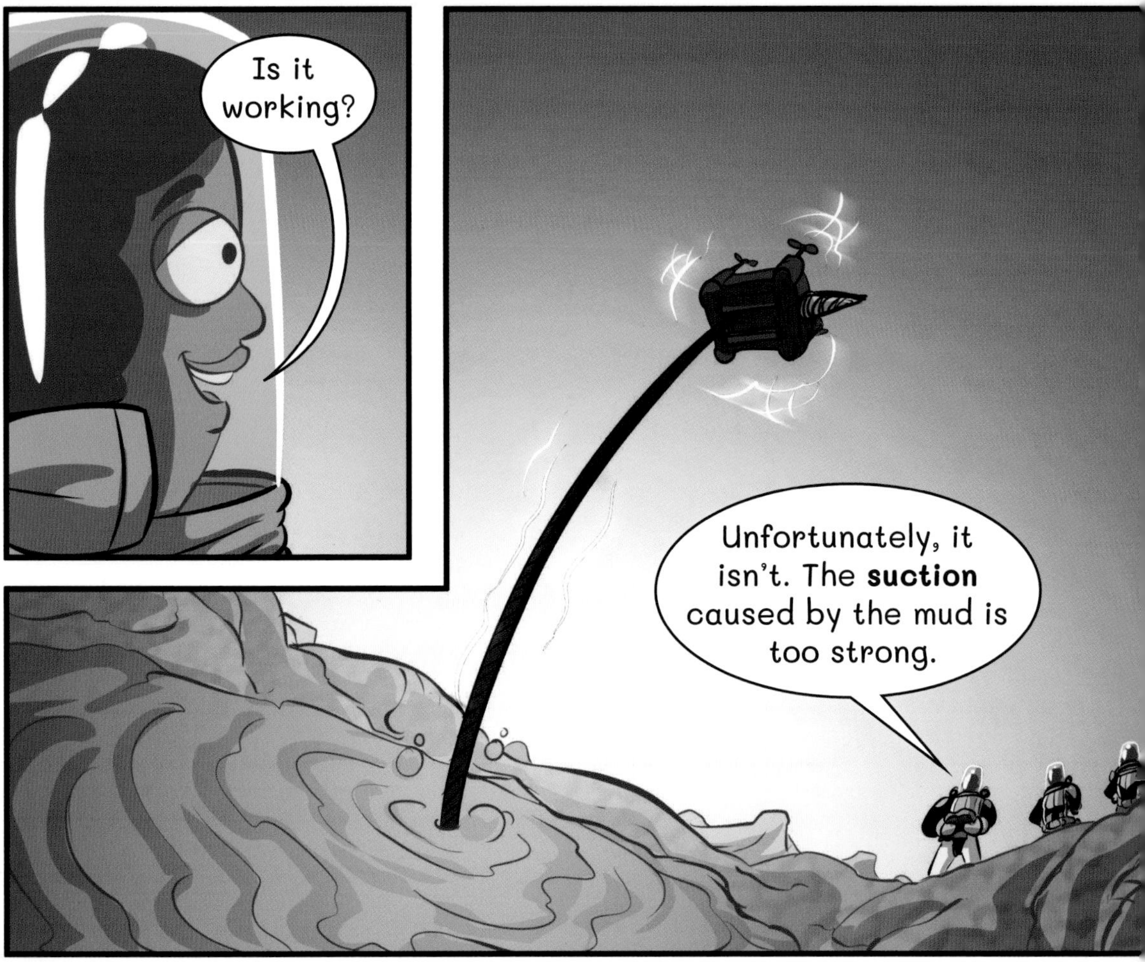
Is it working?
Unfortunately, it isn't. The **suction** caused by the mud is too strong.

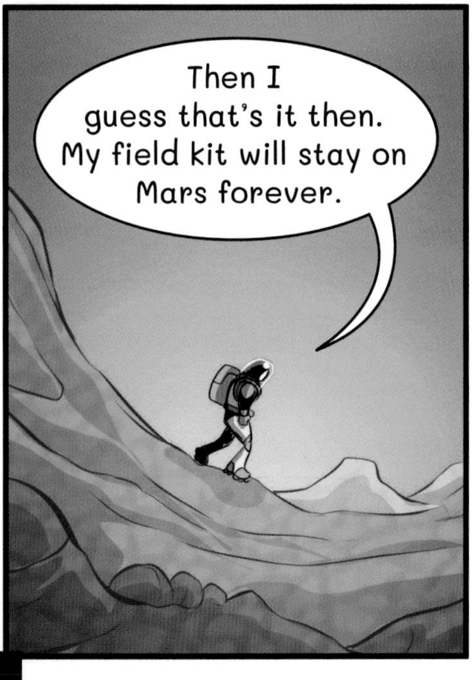
Then I guess that's it then. My field kit will stay on Mars forever.

SCIENCE FACT

Not every piece of equipment sent to spa makes it back home. There are more than 500,000 pieces of "space junk" orbiting E This includes discarded mission-related debris, such as abandoned spacecraft an other equipment.

suction: a vacuum caused by air pressure

THE SCIENCE OF SCIENCE FICTION

Space junk needs to be monitored for the safety of future missions. It is extremely important work. Let's take a look at how it's done!

•It is the job of the Department of Defense to monitor all space trash in orbit.

•The Department of Defense was founded in 1947. It is the largest government agency in the United States.

•The Department of Defense catalogs all space junk larger than a softball.

•There are currently 27,000 objects cataloged.

•While in orbit, space junk travels at speeds up to 17,500 miles (28,164 km) per hour.

•Even something as small as a paint chip could damage a spacecraft.

•Space junk should be avoided. Extensive planning is needed to fly around it. Spacecraft are built with special shields for protection.

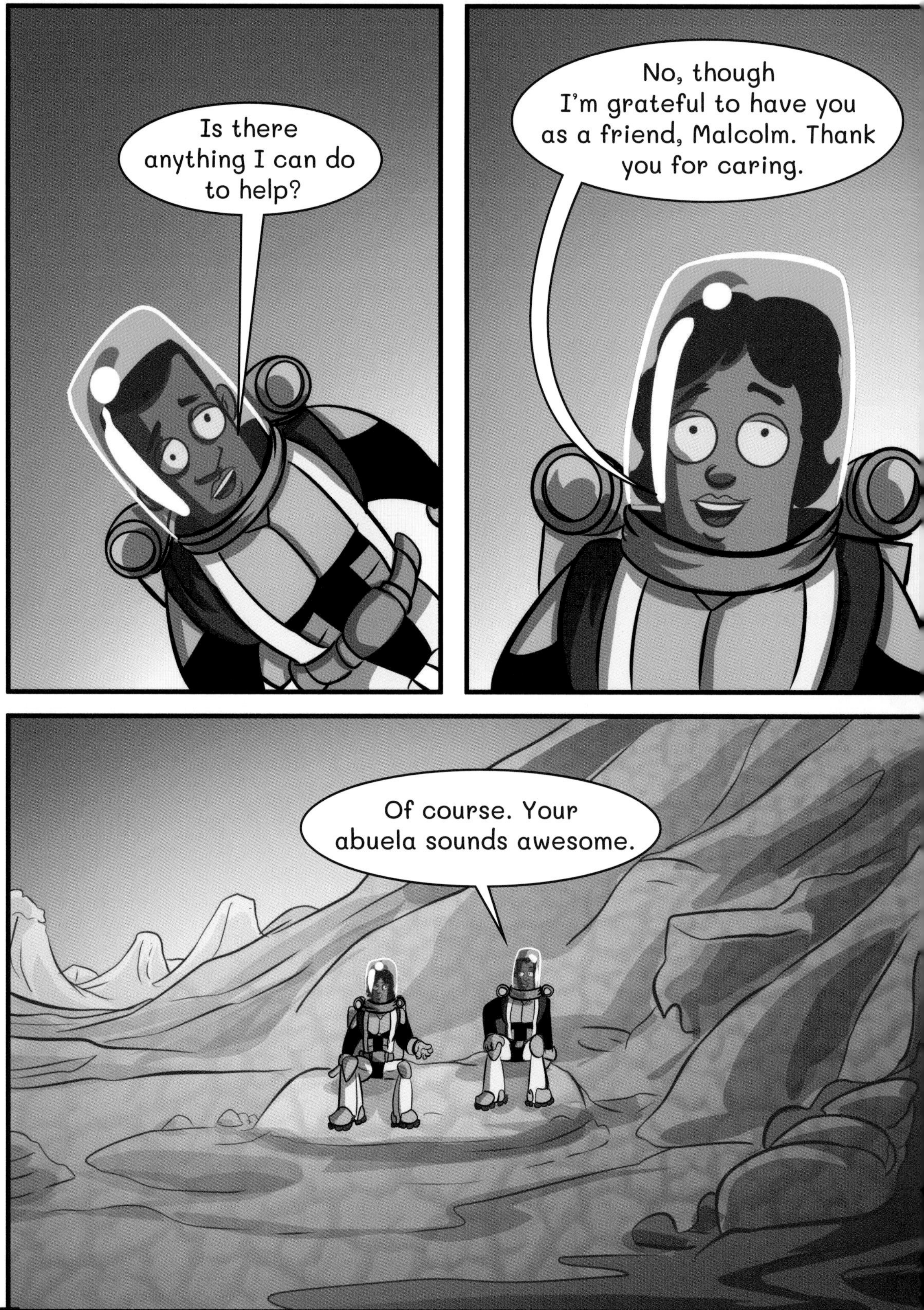
Is there anything I can do to help?
No, though I'm grateful to have you as a friend, Malcolm. Thank you for caring.
Of course. Your abuela sounds awesome.

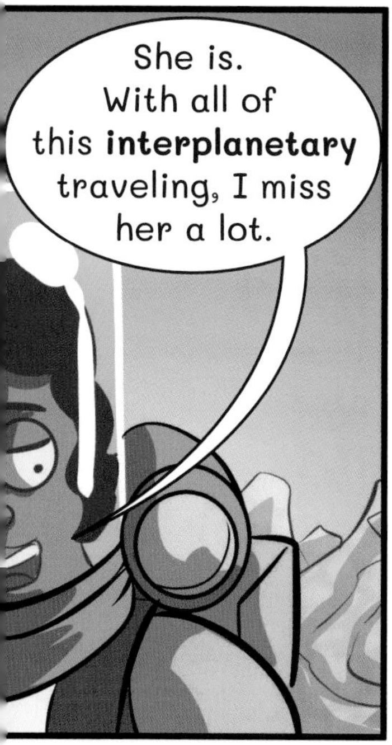
She is. With all of this **interplanetary** traveling, I miss her a lot.

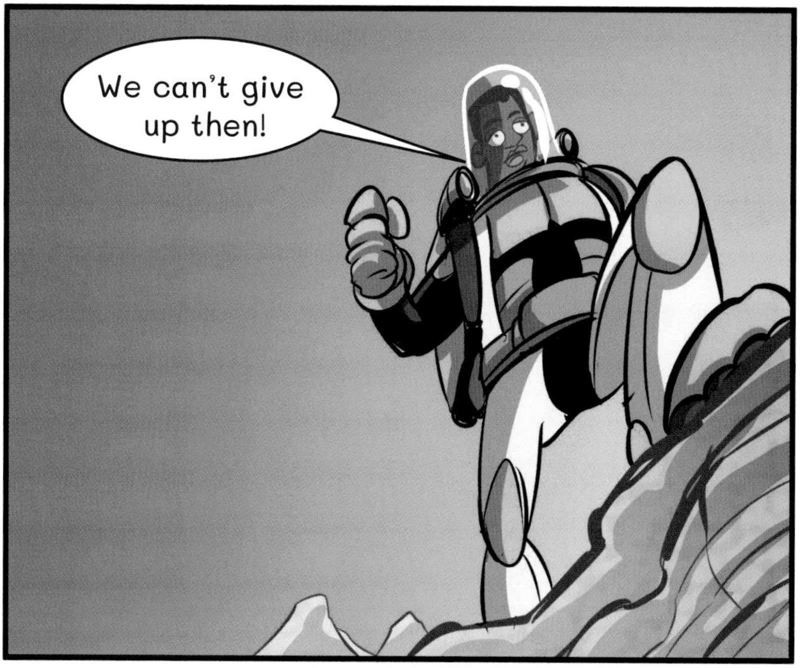
We can't give up then!

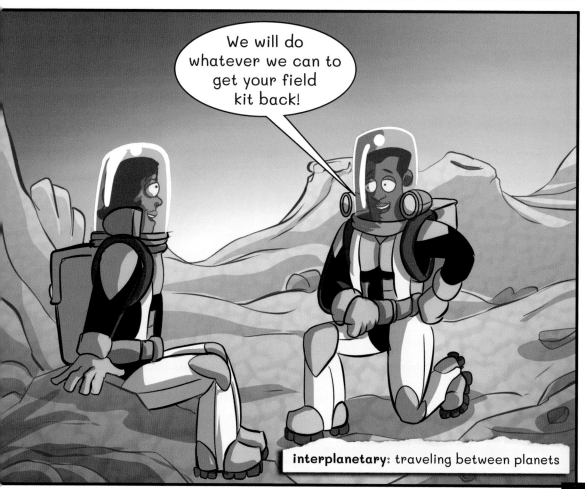

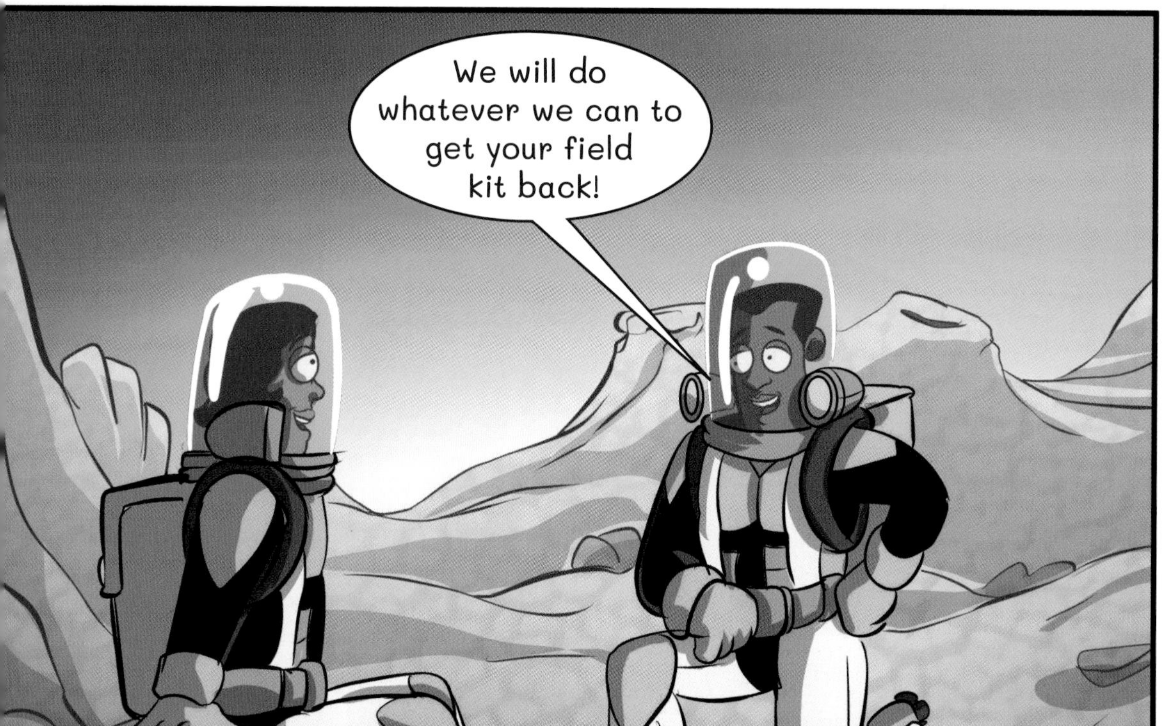
We will do whatever we can to get your field kit back!
interplanetary: traveling between planets

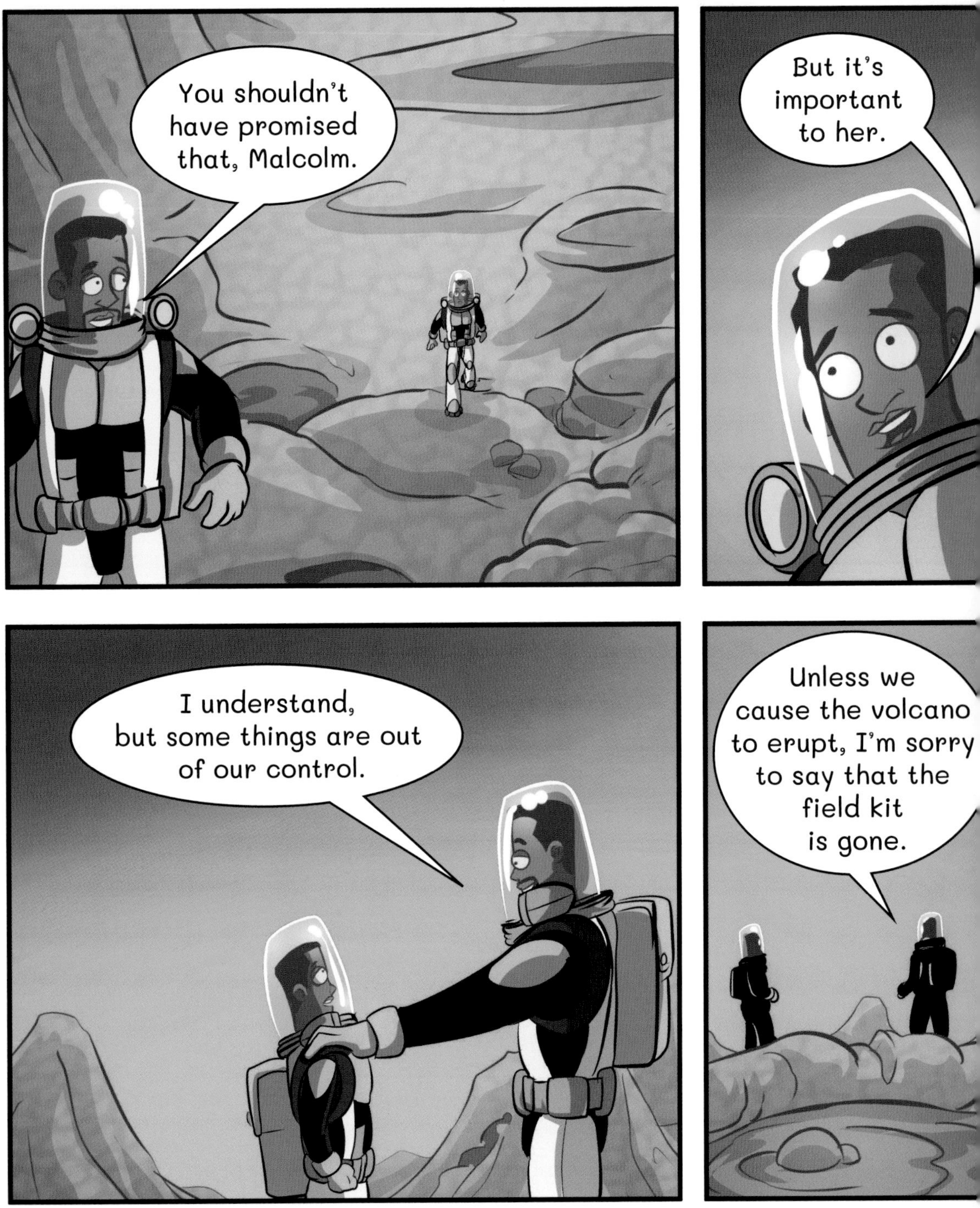
You shouldn't have promised that, Malcolm.
But it's important to her.
I understand, but some things are out of our control.
Unless we cause the volcano to erupt, I'm sorry to say that the field kit is gone.

SCIENCE FACT

Scientists who study volcanoes are called volcanologists. They study how and why volcanoes erupt. They also predict future eruptions, and figure out how the eruptio impact their surroundings.

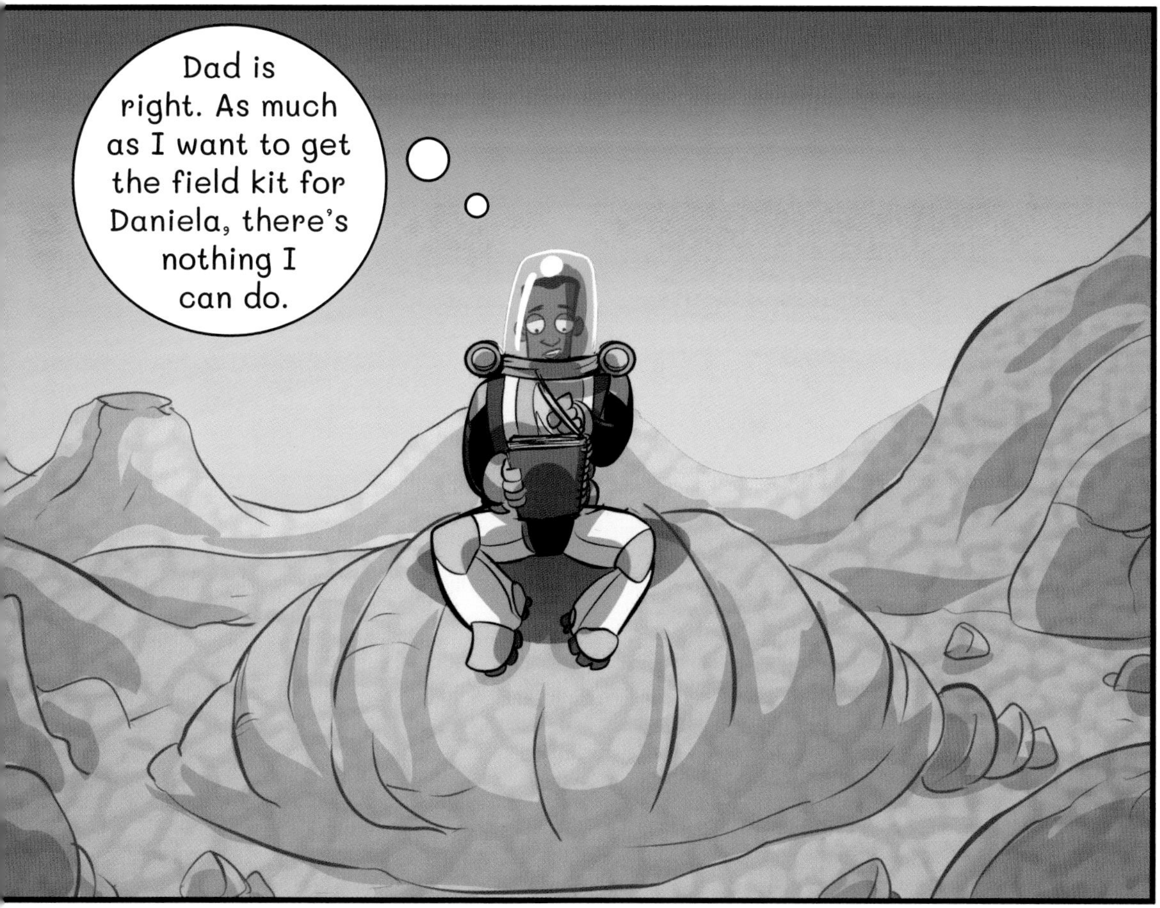
Dad is right. As much as I want to get the field kit for Daniela, there's nothing I can do.

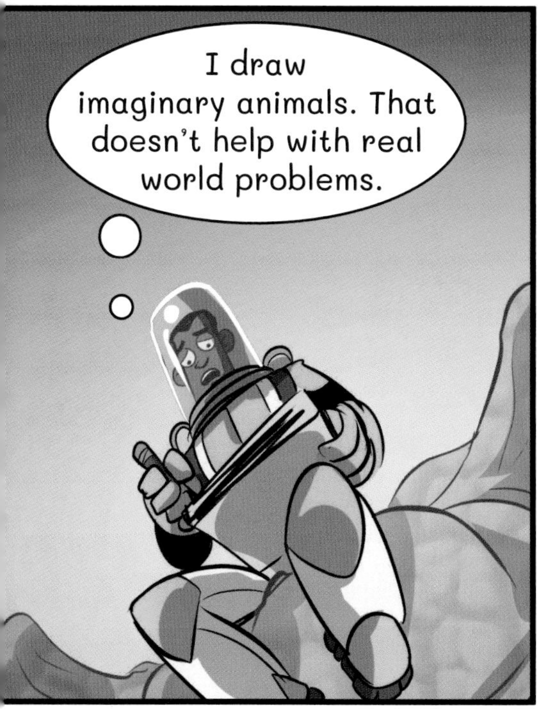
I draw imaginary animals. That doesn't help with real world problems.

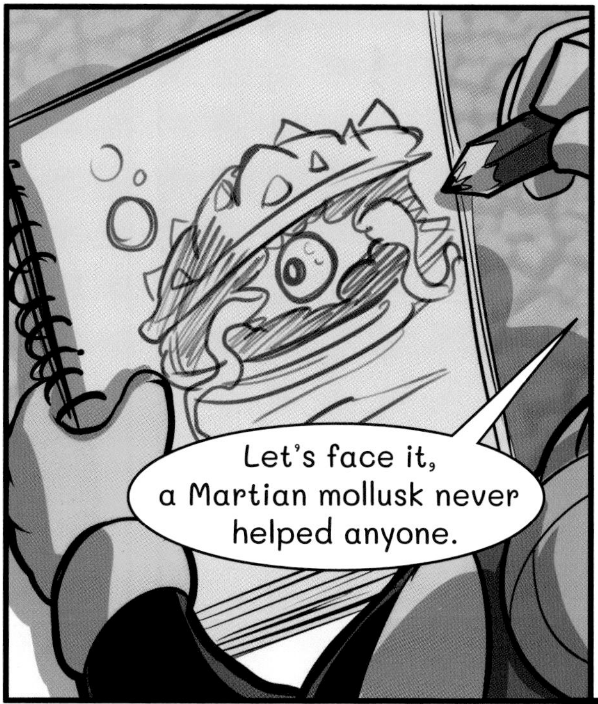
Let's face it, a Martian mollusk never helped anyone.

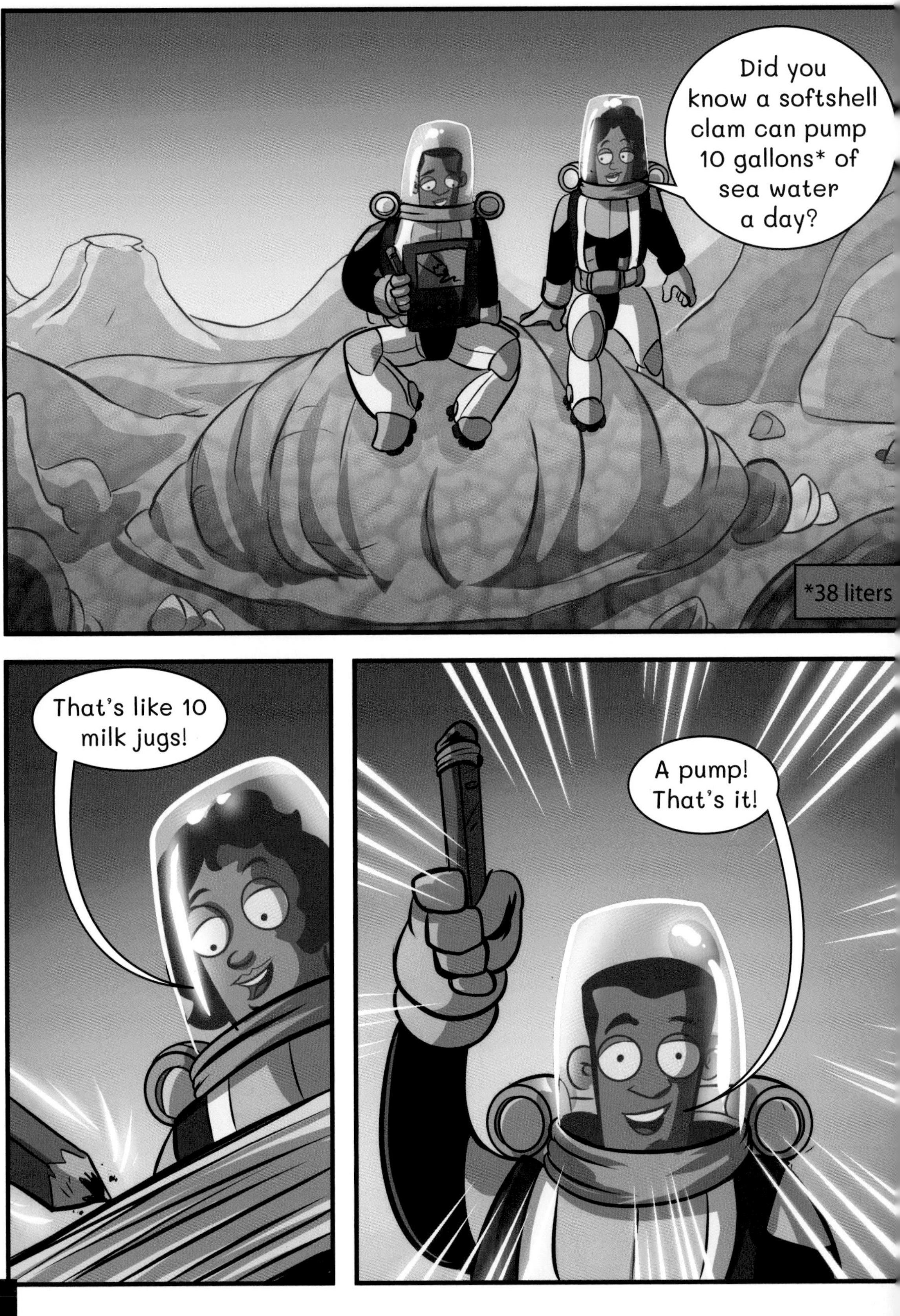
Did you know a softshell clam can pump 10 gallons* of sea water a day?
*38 liters
That's like 10 milk jugs!
A pump! That's it!

THE FUNDAMENTALS OF ART

Let's put the FUN in the fundamentals of art by looking at composition. Composition is the arrangement of the things we see on a page. Review these 2 examples of crabs. How does their placement alter your perception of the image?

•Think of how everything you have drawn works together. This is composition.

•There are many parts of composition. One of them is balance.

•You may want both sides of your image to have the same importance. This is called symmetrical balance. Each side is equally weighted.

•All the parts of the image should work together to create the bigger picture. This is called rhythm.

•Rhythm helps the viewer's eye travel through an image as if it were telling a story.

•Composition is important in art. It impacts how we understand what we see. Changing 1 element in comparison to another can completely alter how it is seen. Drawing something bigger or smaller can make it seem more or less important.

ARTIST TIP: Try drawing 5 different-sized objects on paper. Now cut them out. Next, move them around on a new blank piece of paper to create a scene. Notice how changing the placement of the objects can make you see things in a different way.

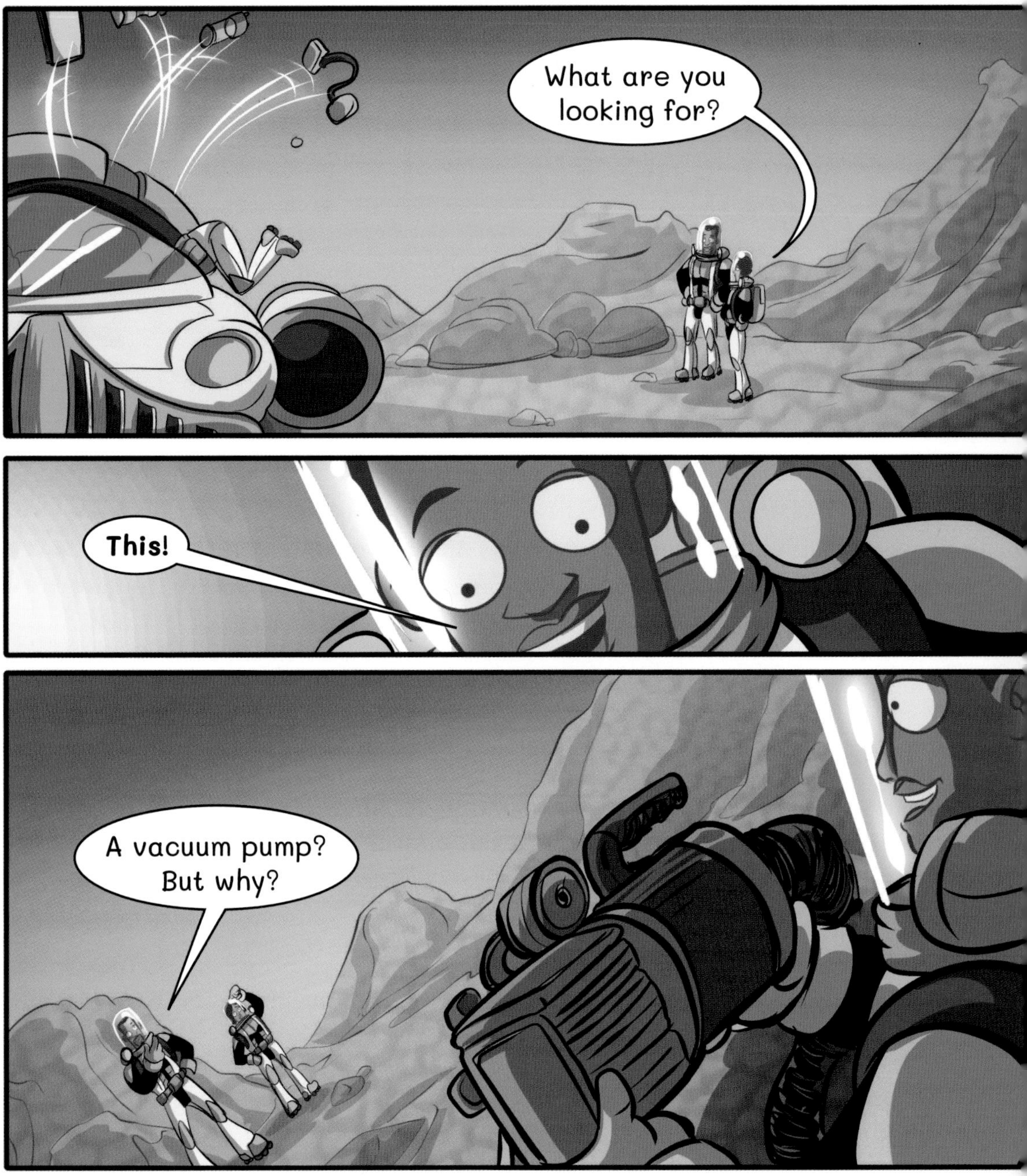
What are you looking for?
This!
A vacuum pump? But why?

MARS FACT

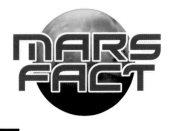

The rovers on Mars take samples of the Red Planet. A tool called a mass spectrometer helps researche look at the samples' makeup. But before they can b studied, they must be ionized. Ionization turns neutral atoms into electrically charged atoms. Ionization can only happen in low pressure conditic Miniature vacuum pumps inside the rover create those conditions.

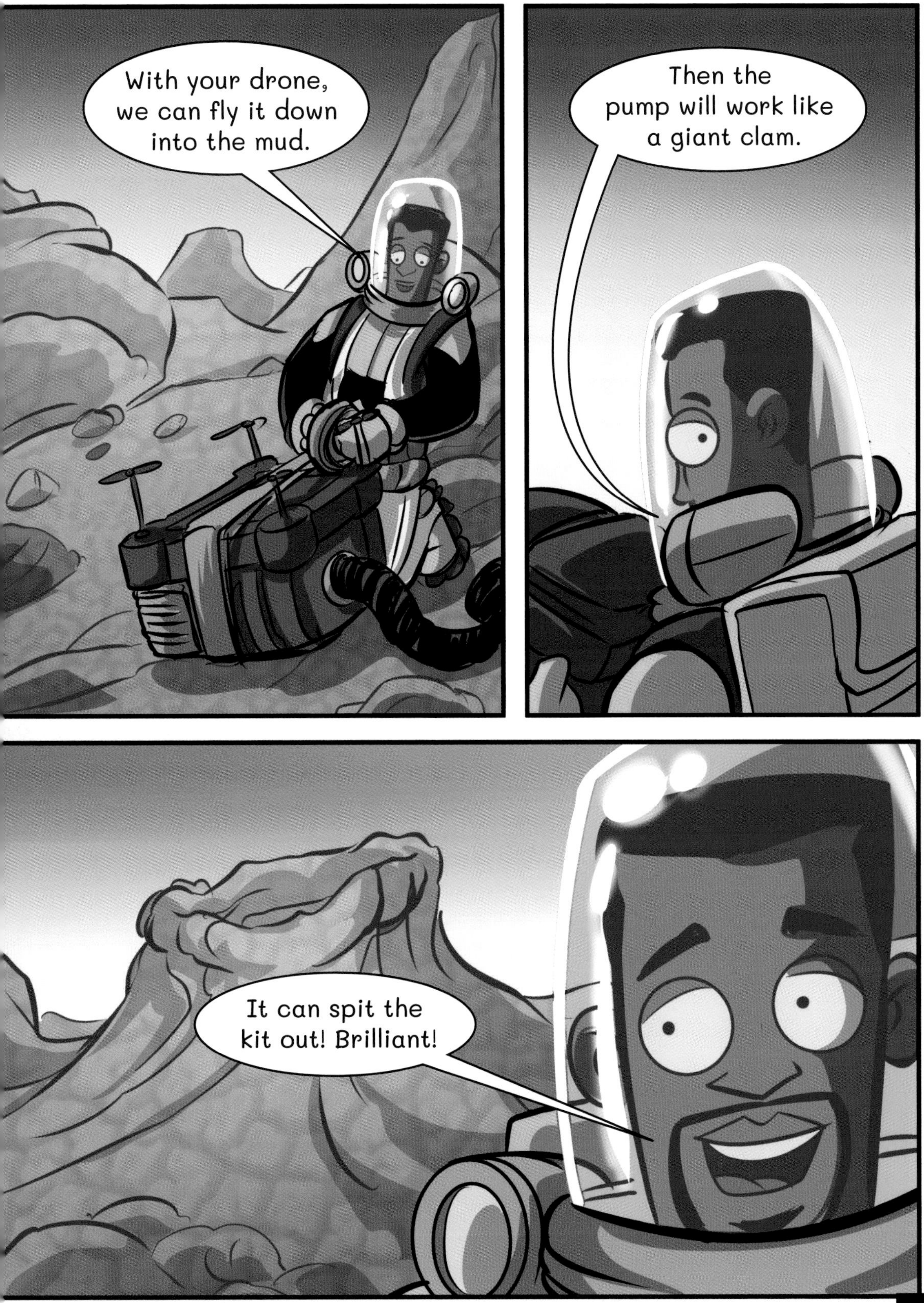
With your drone, we can fly it down into the mud.
Then the pump will work like a giant clam.
It can spit the kit out! Brilliant!

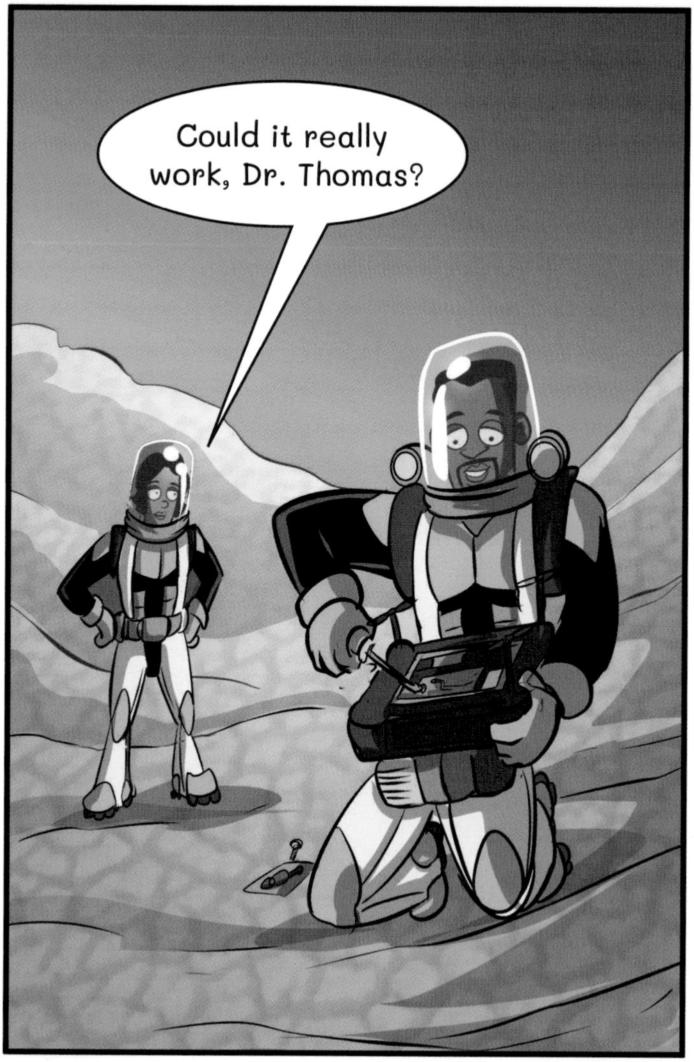
Could it really work, Dr. Thomas?

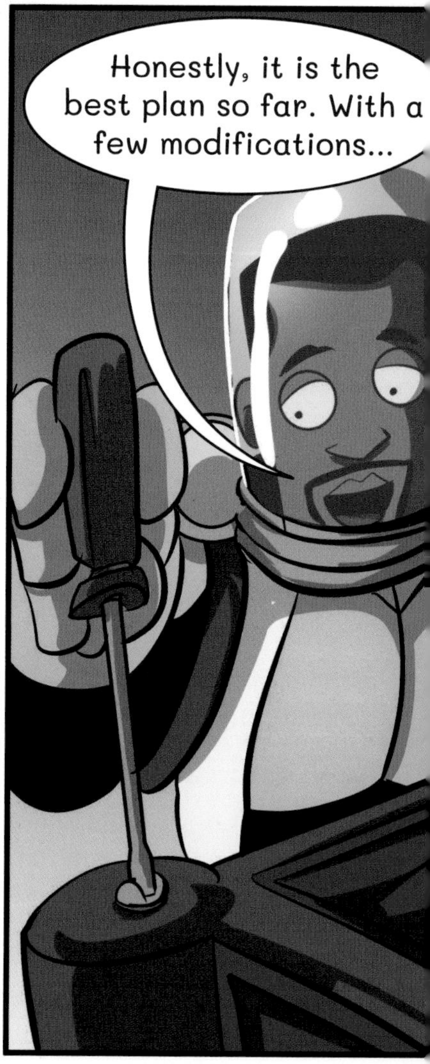
Honestly, it is the best plan so far. With a few modifications...

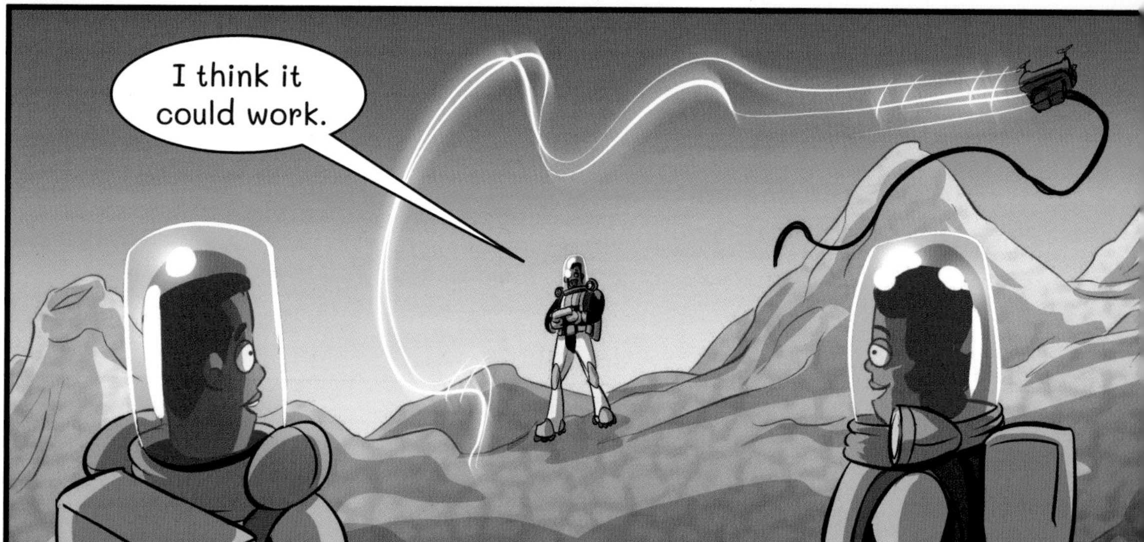
I think it could work.

MARS SURVIVAL TIPS

Not all of the volcanoes on Mars spit mud. Some, like those on Earth, spew lava. Here are some tips for surviving a volcanic eruption, no matter which planet you are on.

- If you find yourself standing next to an active volcano, the first step is to **evacuate**.
- Take only essential items with you. That includes food, water, a first aid kit, a fire extinguisher, and medication.
- Follow evacuation routes. Some areas may be blocked by lava and debris.
- If you can't evacuate, seek shelter immediately.
- Seal off the shelter. Close all windows and doors.
- Go to an interior location of the shelter that is above ground.
- The air will be harmful to breathe. Stay indoors while ash is falling or wear a protective mask.

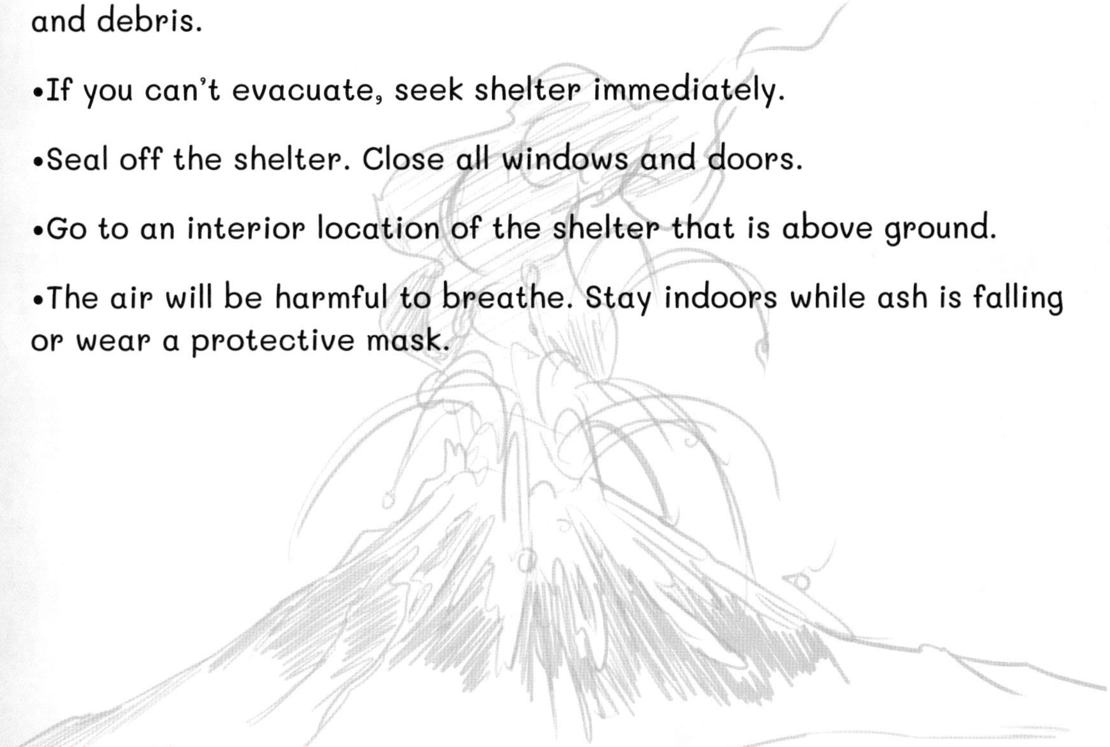

evacuate: move from a dangerous place to a safer place

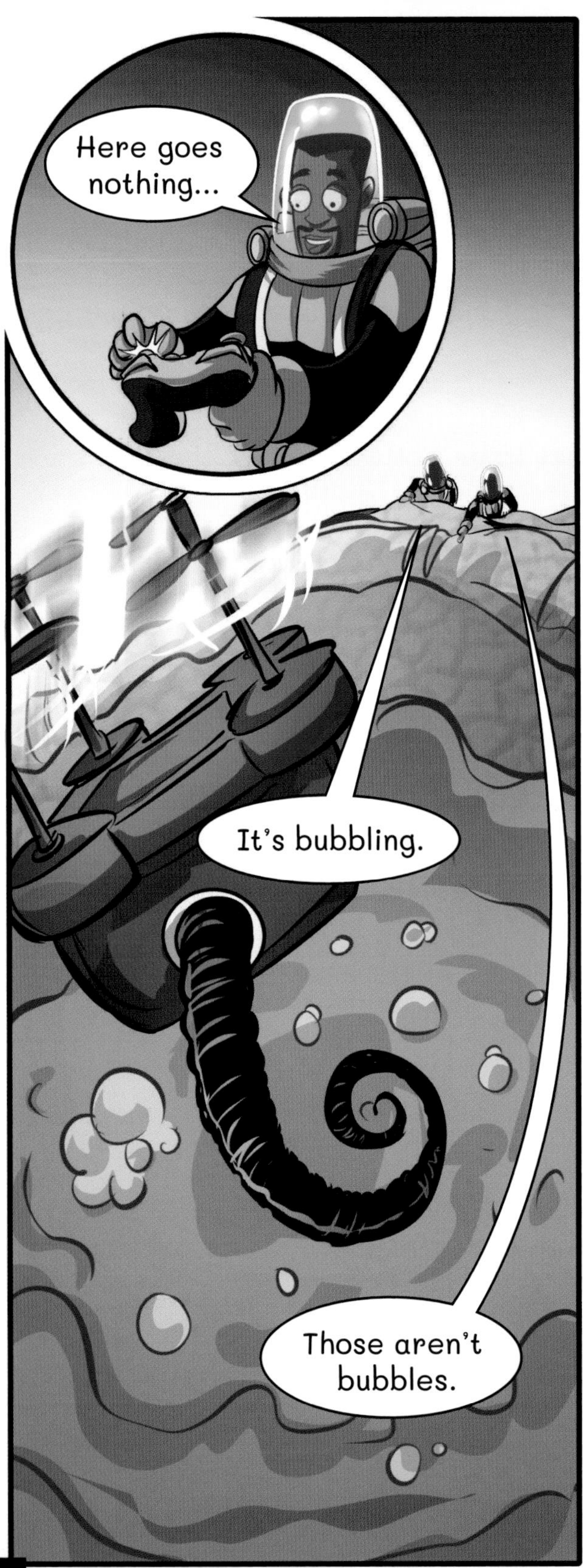
Here goes nothing...
It's bubbling.
Those aren't bubbles.
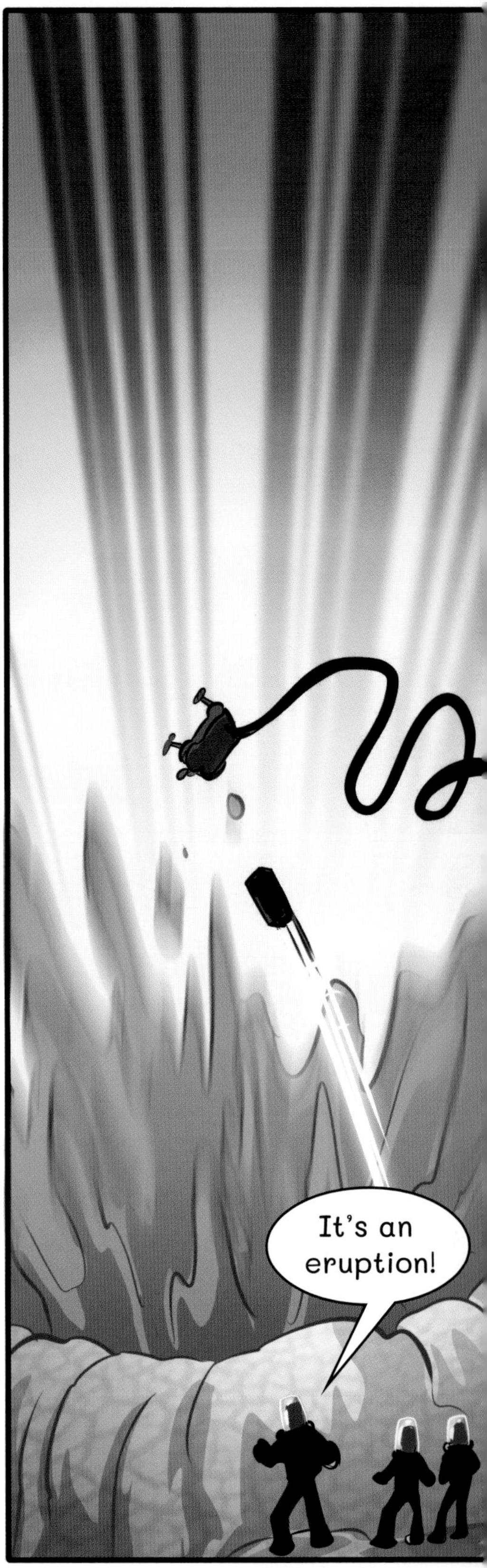
It's an eruption!

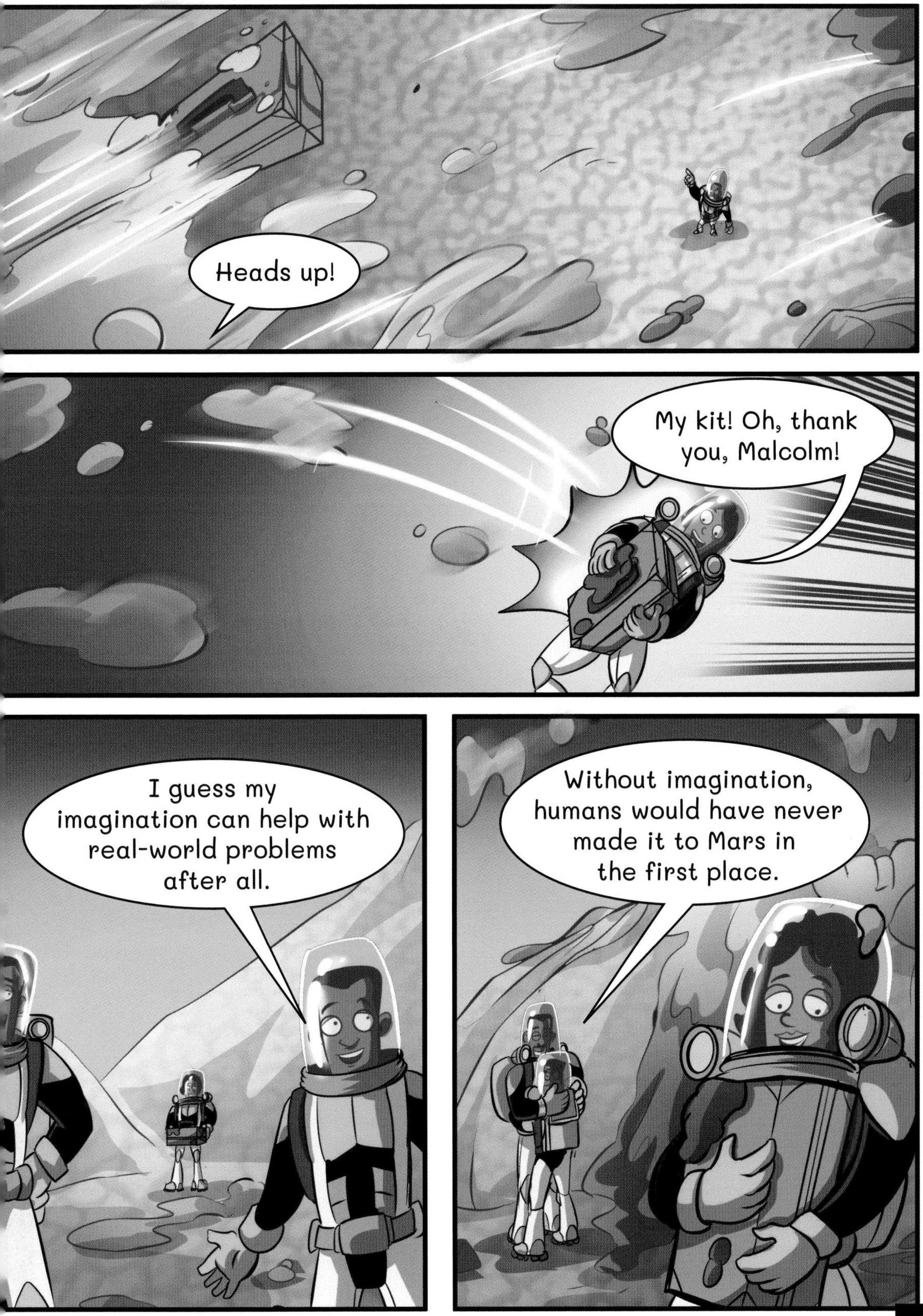
Heads up!
My kit! Oh, thank you, Malcolm!
I guess my imagination can help with real-world problems after all.
Without imagination, humans would have never made it to Mars in the first place.

INDOOR VOLCANO

Daniela almost lost her field kit in the belly of a Mars mud volcano. Thanks to Malcolm, his creativity, and an eruption, the field kit was saved. You can craft your own erupting structure with just a few item found in your kitchen.

WHAT YOU NEED

- glass bottle
- air-dry clay
- a shallow pan
- food coloring
- dish soap
- 2 cups (0.5 liters) water
- 2 tablespoons (30 milliliters) baking soda
- vinegar

STEPS TO TAKE

1. You may make a bit of a mess. Be sure to pick a place that is suitab for the experiment.

2. Sculpt a volcano around the glass bottle using the air-dry clay. Mak sure you leave the opening of the bottle uncovered. Place the volcanc in the shallow pan.

3. Mix the food coloring and a few drops of dish soap with the water. Use your favorite color or add them together to make new colors.

4. Pour the mixture into the bottle at the center of your volcano.

5. Next, pour the baking soda into the bottle.

6. Finally, pour vinegar into the volcano. Watch as the eruption occurs

LEARN MORE

BOOKS

Bolte, Mari. *Exploring Mars*. Ann Arbor, MI: Cherry Lake Publishing, 2022.

Huddleston, Emma. *Explore the Planets*. Minneapolis, MN: ABDO Publishing, a division of ABDO, 2021.

WEBSITES

Mission to Mars!
https://www.mensaforkids.org/teach/lesson-plans/mission-to-mars

Sending humans to Mars is sounding more and more possible. Research the risks and rewards behind the mission.

The Planetary Society: Every Mission to Mars, Ever
https://www.planetary.org/space-missions/every-mars-mission

Where have we sent rovers? Find out where and if they're still operating.

THE MARTIANS

MARTIAN MOLLUSKS

A resident of the mud volcanoes, Malcolm imagines these Martian mollusks can pump mud throughout their own bodies.

GIRAFOPODS

Part isopod and part giraffe, Malcolm imagines this Martian can search the mud volcanoes of Mars with its plate-covered head and neck.

MASON CRABS

Perfectly adapted to Martian mud volcanoes, Malcolm invents these Martians and their beaver-like tails as a way to flip mud around.

GLOSSARY

abuela (uh-BWAY-luh) grandma in Spanish

atmospheric pressure (at-mus-FEE-rik PRESS-shuhr) the amount of air pressure found on a planet

drone (DROHN) a small flying vehicle that is controlled from the ground

evacuate (uh-VAK-yoo-ayt) move from a dangerous place to a safer place

hemisphere (HEM-iss-feer) the top or bottom half of a planet

interplanetary (in-tuhr-PLAN-uh-tehr-ee) traveling between planets

mimicked (MIM-iked) imitated

mud volcanoes (MUD vol-KAY-nohz) vents in the ground that erupts hot mud

multi-functional (MUL-tie-FUNG-shuhn-uhl) capable of performing various tasks

suction (SUK-shuhn) a vacuum caused by air pressure

theories (THEE-reez) ideas used to explain something

wasteland (WAYST-land) an unused area of land that has been neglected

INDEX